THE TEDDY BEARS' PARTY

Elaine Bailey

ream Time Tales

Gemma was feeling miserable. She had been invited to Jenny's birthday party, which was being held that day. Unfortunately, she had caught measles from her younger brother, David, so she was unable to go.

First published 1991.
Published by Peter Haddock Ltd. Bridlington, England.
© Elaine Bailey
Printed and bound in the United Kingdom.

Teddy was there to comfort her, and with him lying by her side she drifted into a deep, deep sleep.

Suddenly, Gemma found herself with David in a large field surrounded by teddy bears. They were cheering loudly as some of the teddy bears ran in an egg and spoon race. Much to her surprise, Gemma's very own Teddy was in the lead, and she and David gave a loud cheer when he won.

After his success, Teddy was very eager to join in the next race, which was the sack race. Once again he was in the lead, but this time he fell over and the little brown bear who was in second position came first.

Because Gemma and David were special guests, they were asked to judge the fancy dress competition. All the bears were dressed in lovely costumes, but finally Gemma chose the little bear who was dressed as a clown.

Much to their dismay, Gemma and David were asked to judge the most beautiful baby teddy bear competition. They found it very difficult to choose one little bear as the winner because they were all beautiful. Eventually Gemma and David decided that they were all winners.

While the fancy dress and baby bear competitions were taking place, Gemma co[uld] see a number of the younger bears on Buttercup Hill enjoying themselves playing leapfrog.

In the next field, which was called Daisy Meadow, a number of bears were swinging high on swings which were tied in a tree and two little bears were going up and down on a see-saw.

Suddenly, Gemma heard a bell ringing. It was tea time. David and Teddy went to one table, where there was pink blancmange and strawberry jelly. Gemma walked across to the other table, where her favourite sandwiches and chocolate chip biscuits were.

Then they all sat down on brightly coloured cloths on the grass to eat their tea. Gemma ate her honey sandwiches and chocolate chip cookies and afterwards drank her cool orange juice.

Then Gemma heard a church clock in the distance striking six. At once all the bears began to tidy up and get ready to go home. The younger bears were very tired, but before they set off home every one of them thanked Gemma and David for coming to their party.

Gemma, David and Teddy began to feel very tired after such an exciting afternoon. They found a large tree which Teddy decided to climb. Gemma and David soon fell fast asleep while the sun set over the fields in the distance.

But when Gemma awoke from her sleep, she found herself tucked up safely in her own bed in her very own little bedroom. She felt much better, and when she looked down at her arms and hands the measles spots had all disappeared.

She hugged Teddy, but she felt something tickling her toes under her duvet. She quickly jumped out of bed, and, she and Teddy looked under the duvet cover. Much to their surprise, there in a little heap were some chocolate chip cookie crumbs. Gemma looked very puzzled. "Now I wonder how they came to be there?" she said with a smile on her face. "Perhaps it was not a dream after all."